DISNEY · PIXAR

THE GOOD DINOSAUR

Adapted by	Illustrated by	Designed by
Bill Scollon	**Michaelangelo Rocco**	**Tony Fejeran**

A GOLDEN BOOK · NEW YORK

randomhousekids.com

ISBN 978-0-7364-3080-7 (trade) — ISBN 978-0-7364-3202-3 (ebook)

Printed in the United States of America

1 0 9 8 7 6 5 4 3 2

Arlo lived on a farm with his family at the base of Clawtooth Mountain.

The little dinosaur was eager to help out so he could add his footprint to the family silo, but he was easily frightened—of everything! Still, Poppa was sure his son would one day earn his mark.

But when Poppa suddenly passed away, Arlo felt **lost**.
Without Poppa's help, how could Arlo ever make his mark?

Life on the farm was hard. The family **struggled** to harvest their crops before the start of winter.

One day, Arlo saw a **critter** taking the family's food. Arlo knew Poppa would have wanted him to scare the critter away. That's how he could **earn his mark** on the silo.

Arlo chased after the
critic. The two struggled,
and Arlo fell into the river!
Arlo **tumbled over and
over** in the rushing
water . . .

. . . and finally washed ashore
far from home.
    Arlo was alone and scared.
But he remembered Poppa saying
that he could always **follow the
river home.**

Arlo began to walk along the winding river. He was **tired and hungry**.

The critter appeared again, and it had brought him **fresh berries**. They were delicious!

The critter and Arlo soon became friends. They had **fun** together, blowing gophers out of holes, and they took care of each other as they tried to find their way home. Arlo named the critter **Spot**.

One night, Arlo ran through a meadow of tall grass. Hundreds of **flickering fireflies** rose into the sky!

Arlo had learned all about fireflies from Poppa.

He missed Poppa a lot.
Spot understood how
Arlo felt. Spot had **lost
his family,** too.

The two **friends**
were glad they had
each other.

The next day, Arlo
and Spot continued on
their way.

Suddenly, a pack of **PTERODACTYLS** attacked them!

Three fearsome **T. rexes** roared and scared the Pterodactyls away.

Would they **attack** Arlo and Spot, too?

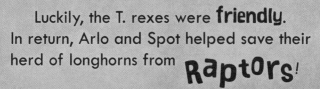

Luckily, the T. rexes were **friendly**. In return, Arlo and Spot helped save their herd of longhorns from **Raptors**!

Later, around a campfire, the T. rexes told Arlo he'd shown **real grit**. Arlo had been scared, but he had proved that he was brave.

He was proud of himself. Poppa would
have been **proud** of him, too.

The next day, Arlo saw **Clawtooth Mountain**!
He was almost **home**! Arlo couldn't wait for his
family to meet Spot.

But the Pterodactyls **attacked** again.
They grabbed Spot and flew away!
Arlo tracked them to the river and
roared a mighty roar, scaring
them away for good.

A big storm was brewing, and Spot
was soon caught in a **flood**. Arlo jumped
into the river to save his friend.

Arlo held Spot tight as they

P
l
u
n
g
e
d

over a
waterfall!

The two friends came to shore at the base
of the falls. They were safe, and Arlo was glad
that their **journey** would soon be over.

As Arlo and Spot went over the mountain pass, a **human family** came into view. Spot was **curious** and went to them.

Arlo knew what he had to do.

The dinosaur drew a **big circle** around all the humans. This would be Spot's **new family**.

Arlo was sad to say **goodbye** to his friend . . .

. . . but he had to **let him go**.

Spot was where
he **belonged**.
And that made Arlo
happy.

Soon, Arlo was where he belonged, too, back on the **farm** with his **family**.

Arlo had found his way home, and he knew he had **earned his mark**.

Poppa would have been very proud.